P9-BZD-984

Also by Tedd Arnold

Dirty Gert

★ "The text . . . [is] as delightful as Arnold's bold, comical
artwork, which is full of brimming, grimy presence."
—*Kirkus Reviews* (starred review)

Fix This Mess!

by
Tedd
Arnold

I Like to Read®

Holiday House / New York

Faith Hamlin, this one's for you!

I LIKE TO READ is a registered trademark of Holiday House, Inc.

Copyright © 2014 by Tedd Arnold
All Rights Reserved
HOLIDAY HOUSE is registered in the U.S. Patent and Trademark Office.
Printed and Bound in May 2014 at Tien Wah Press, Johor Bahru, Johor, Malaysia.
The artwork was created on a Wacom Cintiq monitor using Photoshop.
www.holidayhouse.com

3 5 7 9 10 8 6 4 2

Library of Congress Cataloging-in-Publication Data
Arnold, Tedd, author, illustrator.
Fix this mess! / Tedd Arnold. — First edition.
pages cm. — (I like to read)
Summary: Robug tries to obey when Jake instructs it to
"Fix this mess!" but somehow manages to make things worse.
ISBN 978-0-8234-2942-4 (hardcover)
[1. Orderliness—Fiction. 2. Robots—Fiction.] I. Title.
PZ7.A7379Fix 2014
[E]—dc23
2013009565

Robug came in a box.

Jake turned it on.

"I am ready," said Robug.

"Yes, yes, yes," said Jake. "Fix this mess."

"I will fix this mess!" said Robug.

"No, no, no," said Jake. "Fix this mess!"

"I will fix this mess," said Robug.

"No, no, no," said Jake. "Get rid of this mess!"

"I will get rid of this mess," said Robug.

"No, no, no," said Jake. "Put it all back!"

"I will put it all back," said Robug.

"Okay, okay, okay," said Jake.

"I will fix this mess,"

said Robug.

"Jake missed a spot," said Robug.

You will like these too!

The Big Fib by Tim Hamilton

Dinosaurs Don't, Dinosaurs Do
by Steve Björkman

Fish Had a Wish by Michael Garland
Kirkus Reviews Best Children's Books list
and Top 25 Children's Books list

I Said, "Bed!" by Bruce Degen

I Will Try by Marilyn Janovitz

Look! by Ted Lewin

Pete Won't Eat by Emily Arnold McCully

See Me Run by Paul Meisel
A Theodor Seuss Geisel Award Honor Book

See more I Like to Read books.
Go to www.holidayhouse.com/I-Like-to-Read/